FIRST STORY

First Story changes lives through writing.

We believe that writing can transform lives, and that there is dignity and power in every young person's story.

First Story brings talented, professional writers into secondary schools serving low-income communities to work with teachers and students to foster creativity and communication skills. By helping students find their voices through intensive, fun programmes, First Story raises aspirations and gives students the skills and confidence to achieve them.

For more information and details of how to support First Story, see www.firststory.org.uk or contact us at info@firststory.org.uk.

Can't Touch Our Words
ISBN 978-0-85748-146-7

Published by First Story Limited
www.firststory.org.uk
Sixth Floor
2 Seething Lane
London
EC3N 4AT

Typesetting: Avon DataSet Ltd
Cover Designer: Jeremy Hopes
Printed in the UK by Intype Libra Ltd

First Story is a registered charity number 1122939 and a private company limited by guarantee incorporated in England with number 06487410. First Story is a business name of First Story Limited.

Can't Touch Our Words

An Anthology

By The First Story Group
At Forest Gate Community School

Edited and introduced by Anthony Anaxagorou | 2015

As Patron of First Story I am delighted that it continues to foster and inspire the creativity and talent of young people in challenging secondary schools.

I firmly believe that nurturing a passion for reading and writing is vital to the health of our country. I am therefore greatly encouraged to know that young people in this school – and across the country – have been meeting each week throughout the year in order to write together.

I send my warmest congratulations to everybody who is published in this anthology.

Camilla

HRH The Duchess of Cornwall

Thank You

Melanie Curtis at **Avon DataSet** for her overwhelming support for First Story and for giving her time in typesetting this anthology.

Jeremy Hopes for designing the cover of this anthology.

Intype Libra for printing this anthology at a discounted rate; **Tony Chapman** and **Moya Birchall** at Intype Libra for their advice.

HRH The Duchess of Cornwall, Patron of First Story.

Thanks to:
Arts Council England, Authors' Licensing and Collecting Society, Jane and Peter Aitken, Tim Bevan and Amy Gadney, Suzanne Brais and Stefan Green, Boots Charitable Trust, the Boutell Bequest, Clifford Chance Foundation, Clore Duffield Foundation, Beth and Michele Colocci, the Danego Charitable Trust, the Dulverton Trust, the Drue Heinz Trust, Edwin Fox Foundation, Gerald Fox, Esmée Fairbairn Foundation, the Thomas Farr Charity, the First Story Events Committee, the First Story First Editions Club, the Robert Gavron Charitable Trust, the Girdlers' Company

Charitable Trust, Give a Book, the Golden Bottle Trust, Goldman Sachs Gives, the Goldsmiths' Company Charity, Kate Harris, the Laura Kinsella Foundation, Kate Kunac-Tabinor, the Lake House Charitable Foundation, John Lyon's Charity, Sir George Martin Trust, Mercers' Company Charitable Foundation, Michael Morpurgo, Old Possum's Practical Trust, Oxford University Press, Philip Pullman, the Pitt Rivers Museum, Psycle Interactive, Laurel and John Rafter, the Sigrid Rausing Trust, Clare Reihill, the Royal Society of Literature, Santander, Neil and Alison Seaton, the Staples Trust, Teach First, the Francis Terry Foundation, Betsy Tobin and Peter Sands, the Trusthouse Charitable Foundation, University College Oxford, Garfield Weston Foundation, Caroline and William Waldegrave, and Walker Books.

Most importantly we would like to thank the students, teachers and writers who have worked so hard to make First Story a success this year, as well as the many individuals and organisations (including those we may have omitted to name) who have given their generous time, support and advice.

Contents

Introduction

Anthony Anaxagorou

Writer-in-Residence

Ursula Le Guin famously observed that the creative adult is the child who has survived. It's often the case for most of us that we begin our lives caught within an unmitigated streak of creative fervour, then as we ascend towards the summits of adulthood something unfair and intractable begins to manifest and take hold. We start to undermine what was once a very necessary and natural part of our being. With an unhealthy dollop of derision we cease to play using the very faculties which introduced us to the world, namely our imaginations.

Part of my job not just as a teacher but also as a writer of poetry is to attempt to preserve that spark which rapidly diminishes over time. This is my second year now working at Forest Gate; the group is a slightly younger group than those I had last year but nonetheless they still managed to bring a wonderful assortment of approaches to making poetry.

For me all art would be pointless if we weren't able to see ourselves in the very thing being made: therefore my objective is always to devise a set of exercises which can offer the group a platform to launch not only their own ideas, but to capture the very essence of the cultural experience which sustains them. Each week we would work through a new activity. Some were as simple as rewriting a newspaper headline, which would open up a discussion centred around tabloid news reporting, sensationalism and misinformation. Other exercises included responding to a harrowing image of a young Sudanese girl being preyed on by a vulture in the midst of civil war. Then the following week we would look at the more technical sides of poetry, from the syntax of a piece all the way through to enjambment. We'd study the work of contemporary poets who spoke in a plurality which made the writing relevant and weighted, culminating at last in our own versions of the poems we took apart.

One of the most memorable moments was when I gave each student the opening sentence from one of Raymond Carver's most celebrated short stories, asking them to write a continuation from there on. The line itself is wonderfully abstract and odd as it sees a man with one arm trying to sell another man a photograph of his front door. The outcome was brilliant: one of the girls more or less came close to rewriting the actual story, which took both Mr Gilhooly and myself by complete surprise.

To conclude, I would like to say that the poems contained in this anthology offer a glimpse into the world of young people who are just beginning to familiarise themselves with the society that's about to absorb them. Some poems are viscerally apoplectic, others lean towards the more humorous, while others simply search through the tumult in the hope of finding some kind of reasoning. I like to think that's what good poetry does best: offer us a glance at a peculiar world commonly overlooked and unexplored.

Deeqa Salad

Deeqa was born in Somalia in 1999. She was raised in London, England. She joined First Story as she believed that in this way she will widen her expressive horizons. Also, she believes that this will encourage her to take hold of her future pursuits. The reason Deeqa writes is because she wants to transform her thoughts into expressive and capturing words so as to vent. She expresses a little through humour, however sometimes she can get protective about the things she likes. She is a defensive person (I've learnt that the hard way), and you shouldn't have a go at her unless you feel very strong. She is a strong girl with secured life goals.

Can You Guess Who You Think I Am?

I give life to those who need it,
My little symbolism of love and war,
I watch you grow in all your spontaneous air.

But you know that I'm a divergent,
So many want me but yet loved by none,
I crave freedom.

Brave Medics to Get Special Medal

Running whilst the soul hides,
They are not called 'The Brave' for no reason,
Their arch-nemesis Death sneaks out of the midst of finite reality,
'All this will soon end, for your destiny is with me.'

The dance between life and death can be compared to the
Latin tango,
Their sinister waves moving to the drums and guitars of the now.

This heroic deed was told by many,
Of these furious three,
And their superhuman means.

They carry the child home
Whilst the cleverest of them reflects on our slowly breaking
society.

Turning Up Was NEVER My Decision

Turning up was never my decision,
I assure you my friend it cannot be mine.

Walking into my house,
Curiously watching the mysterious night sky,
From attic bedroom's window sill,
Hoping that the view from here wavers my imagination
away from
The acid atmosphere of that mechanical school.

Inside there.
The constant wear and tear physically and mentally drove me
to near insanity,
As the plastic mean girls commence enemy fire at me.
The hands of the universe direct me to this party,
The magic, mayhem and more.
RIIIING…… RIIIING…… RIIIIIIIIING!!!!!
My cell phone calls,
Grown ups' house,
My best friend 'needed' me.

Awoken by flashes of light,
Humanity lies on my sides,
Moving lips make cheering and jeering noises descending from
their mouth.
No amount of alcohol could have wiped away the memory of
these consecutive episodes of that day.

The Misfortunate Earth

Soaring through America, the land of the free,
Forgetting my last stop's sewing machines.
Static sounds and good homes for the rich,
Are where I want to reside in next.

There goes the daily pawnbrokers where the beggars quench the
sweet liqueur from the rich's urine.
Sad story.
The poor really have outdone themselves tonight!
Next stop,
the East-end of Africa,
'watch out for the missiles,' I signal to my companions
'don't want to get your plume feathers damaged, do you!'

Hark! I see an outline of a child on the floor,
surprisingly she has no friends,
I suspect she's crying.
My friend Ash swoops down snapping his beak.

What have I done,
#regret

Scary Opening

Bang! Vanish! What was that thing? A sharp, metallic click scooted through the kitchen. My band posters began to destroy themselves, which in turn opened up a huge vacuum hole. I was in.

Ridhwaanah Khanom

Ridhwaanah is quite hard to describe. She is amazing, caring, a bit mad and has a very dark mind, but that's just Ridhwaanah. Her journey to First Story was a weird one because the first day she came, she ran out the classroom which left a fantastic impression on everyone. Overall, Ridhwaanah is a very talented writer and has a way with words – it's kind of like a secret sauce you may say – she just has no limits. Ridhwaanah also has a very wide imagination, her ideas can be so mad sometimes but she always makes them work. You would be very lucky to meet someone like her.

Society

The solitary giraffe was hungry,
So it found the betraying chocolate,
The animalistic Mars bar terror.

But the wild killer whale was hungry as well
And caused havoc in the peaceful water
The furious fire wanted to burn
So it made pollution on delusional Earth.

The malicious moon shone on the murderous glass
And every one died
So all that was left was an abused corpse.

Honesty Is Not the Best Policy

I've cheated but I have no guilt
They said we could use our own resources
And that fair play is really unfair
So I've won and they've lost
And all is good for now.

I cheated because I made a mistake
A mistake to take actions too slow
I procrastinated too much
And did too little
When I could've ended it all just like that.

I gambled for options
And tried to avoid that one decision
That could make life easier
But could also make it harder
All in good time.

The guilt tried to kill me
It tried tying rope around my neck
Tried to choke me to death
But I easily stopped it because a stupid feeling couldn't crush me
I was indestructible
For now, at least.

I think you are ready
Ready to know the truth
The truth of how I won the game
The truth about how I cheated
And forced the rest to lose
I killed them all, one by one
And made them all suffer
I would stick a knife into their back and twist it round and
round like a merry-go-round
I chopped them up into tiny little pieces and felt happy
doing this.

Because they were good people
And there's always a price to pay for those that try to be heroes
And their dead, staring eyes were like buttons, lifeless
They didn't make me feel sad, or bad, or even mad at myself.

And remember, honest people will never survive in this world
So yes,
I cheated and I have no guilt
Because to be honest
I really don't care.

The Octopus

The octopus shot itself against its rival
Covering his face with its slimy, sticky body
It stuck its venom gland into its enemy's mouth
Letting the poisonous ink pour in.

The octopus watched his prey's life slowly deteriorate
Watched how his body began to change to different colours
 of the rainbow
Red, orange, yellow, green, blue, indigo, violet and finally black.

The attacker's body fell back
With the appearance of nothing
But also with the appearance
Whilst the successful octopus sat there
Without an inch of guilt
Smirking with satisfaction.

Forgotten

She was weak and starving
But I couldn't do anything
She was patient and praying
But I could give her no help.

She clutched at my greasy hair
Using the little amount of energy she had
But it wasn't my fault
Why should I care?
She was just another forgettable child
In a forgettable town
With a forgettable face.

She was the prey but who was the predator,
The photographer, or the vulture,
He looked at me with his magnified eye,
His three legs steady and safe on the ground,
Unlike the little girl,
His owner was reckless and stupid,
Without a care for the poor child's death
But with a care for his money.

The bones and dust lay on my flat panes
I wasn't grateful, but I was hateful
Why did I have to have no moisture?
Why did people constantly die on me?
What had I done to deserve this?
Nothing. I had done nothing because I could do nothing.

The child was waiting, waiting for her time to come
She was vulnerable
Her heavy necklace was dragging her fragile body down
And I could hear her breath drifting away
Until she could breathe no more.

A few minutes later, her flesh was gone, finished
And so was her life
But I didn't care
Because this was what happened every day
So I didn't even bother crying
Because I had no tears left.

Her bones began to sink into my body
Locking any memory of her in me
I thought about the photographer and hoped he had got what he wanted
His foolishness and carelessness had contributed to the poor girl's death
So she was nameless
She was forgotten.

Death Is Not Something to Despise

Before you visit the door of death
You must go through fear
Feel the sadness
And the badness of the world
So you will not be frightened of the lonely and lovely peace
 and sanctity
You may have in the future.

You must feel the pain in your jaws
As you continuously grind your teeth
Grind away at the sorrow
Ponder about your miserable life
With your dysfunctional family
And your broken home.

Where your parents constantly argue
About money, and lying, and deceit
Because that is all that matters to them
And when all the anger reflects on you
You're unable to control yourself
So you become the monster in the house, the 'different' one.

Before you know death properly
You must travel to the hardest parts of the world
Where poverty, starvation and mourning always stay and
 claim territory

You must rely on death as a second-nature
So you will never be afraid
If death comes knocking on your door.

You must see citizens dying
Forever in your mind
Innocent people being cold-bloodedly murdered
So you can always picture it in your conscience
And then you will be able to tell yourself
I am not scared anymore.

You must live in death
Breathe it like the clean air
Rely on it
Like a baby relies on its mother
So when you are on your death bed or a bullet is shooting right
through you
You will be happy
Happy that you're dead.

Unknown

A shadow walking past you
Invisible to your eyes
You never seem to notice me
I didn't know you were so blind.

Stuck in this world
With no sense of direction
Empty. Empty soul
Where did it go?
Where did I go?

I guess you'll never know
Since you can't see me
Frozen hands and frozen eyes
If you keep smiling, the wind will change your features

With designer clothes and your caked face
Walking down the road without a care
But you do care, don't you?
You try to hide it, but I know it's there

You try to run away from the real you
Try to conceal your feelings
And stop the you that is true

So I am the shadow in your way
You see me
But you never really notice me
Strolling by without a care

I used to be like you
Unsure and unheard
Trying my best to fit in
But instead I turned invisible

I asked myself who I am
I was looking for identity.
I felt the silence of my soul.
No answer.

I looked at the stars one by one.
They asked for identity too
So tell me stranger, who am I, and who are you?
We both walk by without a care

Two shadows mould into one
An identity lost, is found
An identity found, is lost
And still we remain invisible
Strolling by without a care
Because now we both know
That neither of us cares.

Nafhat Sharif

Nafhat, a calm quiet girl of Nigerian background, likes to spend her days watching Naruto. She enjoys life and makes a lot of jokes. She gets on with her work and achieves high grades, but she's no geek, she's a popular girl with many friends. Her life is great and there is much, much more.

Nafhat is a part of the Islamic faith and enjoys being part of it. Her days are spent with school, worship, socialising and relaxing. In many ways her life is perfect – is yours?

Hate

Before you know what hate really is
you must experience betrayal,
Have someone rip your beating heart out of your chest
and stomp on it repeatedly until you feel nothing but
numbness.

Hate is like a clay pot,
It has to set for a while before its full potential is shown.

Hate leads you through a maze of emotion,
taunts you,
and traps you at dead ends
but you must fight and push on through.

Before you know what hate really is,
You have to have fallen into the deepest,
darkest
abyss
of unimaginable pain
and not be able to crawl out.

This devil of an emotion unleashes your inner demons and
sometimes
They escape forever.
That's when it all ends and you're no longer in control.
Your mind is not yours.
Your body has betrayed you.
Your heart becomes cold
And that's when it's all
over.

My Sister's Keeper

I awoke at three a.m. to the laughter of my little sister.

She gleefully screamed, 'Timmy, I don't like this game because your hands are always too tight around my neck!'

Lifting the thick black covers off my bare legs, I reluctantly slid out of my bed and tiptoed with caution past the bathroom and to her room. Normally I was absolutely petrified of the dark, but curiosity and worry pummelled my fear.

Wait.

Who was Timmy?

Was he a friend?

Did he sleep over?

How old was he?

All these questions swam like eels in the fish tank that is my brain.

The euphoric laughter had abruptly stopped and so did my rapidly beating heart. As much as I felt the urge to jump into my cocoon of blankets and warmth, my 'big sister senses' tingled and I knew I had to do something.

With every step I took, the old wooden floorboards creaked and the noise echoed throughout the spacious hallway.

I finally reached the baby pink door of my sibling's room. My pale hands shook as I reached for the brass knob. I twisted the cool metal to the right and pushed with all my might.

Entering her room – which was ten degrees warmer than mine – I glanced around only to realise:

It was empty.

The window on the far left was cast open, curtains flailing

vigorously, a bitter gust of wind forcing itself through the opening and sending a shiver down my spine.

My heart dropped to my stomach and I collapsed to the floor in a heap of panic, grief and sorrow.

She was my best friend,
My love,
My only sister,
And now,
She was gone.

The Camera

I don't want to do this.
I can't just stand here helplessly
And let the paper thin flesh of this young girl
Be savagely ripped from her frail body.
But what can I do?
I'm just a useless piece of machinery.
I don't want to do this.
This poor excuse of a man who uses me doesn't have a heart.
I may be just a camera,
But I have more compassion in my battery
Than this monster has in his whole body.
I shouldn't have to do this.
My lens wasn't prepared to witness the gruesome scene in
front of me.
The girl clutches the dry grass with her bony fingers.
It was as if she wanted to spend her last few moments
Grasping desperately onto something that was also dying.
The difference is the grass probably doesn't feel any pain.
She has her whole life ahead of her and I stand here helpless
As she slowly crumbles into the soil.
I never wanted to do this.
But I have no choice.

Sara Munir

Sara Munir was born in 2001 in Pakistan and moved to Britain when she was over a year old. She was raised in London. Sara Munir was just completing an exhilarating year in Debate Mate when she hungered for more self-expression like the way she did in speaking her views previously. Then a school writing club amidst the depths of the literary underground tapped her on the shoulder. Sara was invited to First Story because of her impeccable writing skills and the ability to make words into something more. She chooses to write because she feels like it's good for her future and she feels that she can express herself through writing and poetry. In my words, I have known Sara for quite a while and she is the most understanding, thoughtful person you could ever meet and she never fails to impress, especially when it comes to writing. If you ever come across Sara Munir, stop yourself and listen to her wise words because I did and it's amazing! She enjoys First Story as it helps her build the blocks to her slowly unwinding future.

Touched

I'm the attraction to your eyes,
And the assassination of your soul.
That beauty that pulls you closer,
And then that villainous scene that lets it go.

I'm the heat to your body,
And the death of your foes.
That tender and warmth,
And then that cringiness in your body.

I'm the forfeit of your father,
And possessed by your mother.
That burst of joy,
And then that stab of treachery.

I'm the modern royalty,
And the modern devil.
That touch of pride,
And then that soulless dive.

I'm the boldness of the world,
And one day I'll make it stop

The Figure Behind My Phone

It was horrible. Absolutely ridiculous. A waste of my time. I bashed the front door open. My phone vibrated as heavy tears rolled down my frozen face. I pulled it out of my jeans in anger. 'Hello?' I spoke. There was no reply. 'Hello?' I continued. Frustrated, I cut the phone. My phone vibrated again. 'Hello? Who is this?' I screamed. I heard a faded evil laugh. I cut the phone again assuming that it was a prank call. I chucked my phone onto the couch and ran up to my room. The room deeply fogged up as I stepped in. There was a figure in the corner of my room looking at me as blood poured out of its eyes. My heart skipped a beat.

It limped its way towards me as I froze and stared at it in horror. I was gobsmacked at this horrible truth. Suddenly I realised that it was getting closer and closer. I ran down the stairs and was forcing the door open. It was jammed. I was trapped, all alone, puzzled about what to do. I dashed towards the back door hoping that it was open. As I pulled the handle, it broke. I was petrified, and had gone blank. What shall I do? How should I escape?

THOMP, THOMP, THOMP! I heard that creature make its way down the stairs. I decided to bolt into the living room and lock myself in. So, this is what I did. As I peeped through the keyhole, I saw the creature looking around in search of me. I jumped back. My heart was racing and my eyes were scanning the room like a detective. I saw the window and gravitated towards it. I carefully looked outside, checking if everything was clear. It was clear! I wanted to rejoice but I guess it wasn't the right time...

I grabbed this long metal object and smashed the windows open. I carefully jumped outside but then realised that I had left my phone behind. I went in my house again and took my phone. The creature was bashing this door open. I had a mini heart attack. I zoomed out with my phone and closed the curtains from the outside to stop the creature that was hunting me down. I ran down the street and felt at peace. Then I searched for the hotel that my parents were in.

Surprisingly, there weren't any people on the high street. I was perplexed. Then I realised that there were figures all around the place. I was busted. I began to get emotional again, like my life was over. I found a corner and was wishing goodbye to everything that existed. I had lost all hopes. I rested my head onto my knees and closed my eyes. After a few minutes, I raised my head, surprised that I was still alive.

I looked up and saw in front of me a hero.

Heartless

No, Love isn't about having fights,
Having fights is the foundation of love,
Just like the flour in a cake.
The amount isn't less,
So there will be a lot!
But at the end,
When the cake is ready,
It's sweet!

It's all about the friendship,
The understanding and care,
It's like tying your shoelaces,
With two hands of course,
It's barely possible with one.
It takes quite a bit of effort, but stops you from tripping,
And at the end, it makes your shoes look good!

Loss

It was gone,
Forever lost,
Never returning,
Impossible,
Utterly unbelievable.

The depressed chocolate melted away,
As the shocked chair watched in silence,
What about the dead poster?
It welcomed the chocolate into his gang,
The shocked chair was forever alone.

Ben Drain

A strange life, full of many things from sewing to sci-fi and media studies, to making scrummy food. Ben has an interesting life. He was born in Newham General and spends most of his time at school. On his holidays he stays with his Nan in the countryside and has immense fun. In his spare time after school he likes to watch YouTube stars such as PewDiePie, VSauce, and AwesomeAlanna. He has a wide spectrum of interests, but to relax he loves to write.

Companionship

Companionship is a thing that will take a long time to achieve
There are many different paths, some right, some wrong

For instance, a perilous road is hate
It twists and turns
Taking you through rough fields of corn
And into muddy puddles

Another is lust
Tearing through love and good emotions
You will find it hard
But you will eventually find the right path

Kindness is a great road to hare down
You'll find happiness along this path
The path will be blocked by the tumbleweed of spite
But you will prevail.

Pressure Screws Up Your Identity

You enter a state of pressure
Unable to change
Taking in the crap of society
You fall into the abyss

Your powers to get out are disabled
Stuck in the cycle
Feeling the pressure
Wait, peer pressure

The endless crowds
And the endless opinions
But you can't get rid of them they'll always be there
You die

You sink into a state of depression
Drinking and drugs
Violence and hate
Because you wanted to conform

Your life destroyed
You can't see any hope
Is there any hope?
No

You lie around all day
Feeling sorry for yourself
Missing the life you could have had
But you chose not to have it

You wonder why you chose your life
But the plain answer is
You didn't choose it
It was chosen for you

This all may hurt but it's plain to see
You played your part
You've done it too
You've screwed someone up

But that's life
A never-ending circle that won't help you out
But there could have been hope
If you'd have just listened

Taken the time to pick out the time-wasters
Ignored the opinions and got on with your work
You could have had a better life and a better identity
But you didn't and that's tough, so get lost.

But Why Am I the Bad Guy?

Waiting, waiting, waiting
Will he feed me or her?
He knows that I will eat her
But why am I the bad guy?

If he leaves her under my watchful eye
He knows what will happen
He should be giving her the supplies he has
But why am I the bad guy?

Will he scoop up the future-to-be?
Or will he let her down?
He may leave her and I may eat her
But why am I the bad guy?

The basic things she needs
He has in his truck
Water and some meat
But why am I the bad guy?

A one mile drive what cost is that to him?
Couldn't he save her by taking ten minutes of his life?
To save her from my stomach
But why am I the bad guy?

But why am I the bad guy?

Every Wednesday

If the law was up to me
Every student's face, except mine,
Would be made of pie
Every Wednesday

The reason for this is
Moods would fly to the moon
And soar to the universe's edge
Every Wednesday

It would happen like this…
Every Wednesday

Lining up in a quivering state of fear
Teachers would have pies
For hands
Every Wednesday

Towels are essential
To wipe away the hands
Stopping the pies from ruining their education
Every Wednesday

However once a month the
Pie tables would flip
The pies would be on the underside of the tables – I don't
know why
Every Wednesday
Every Wednesday

I Am a Colour, but What Colour Am I?

I radiate around pain
Making it look worse
I change it to an illness
Infecting the flesh

Swarming around a baby's room
Introducing more love
A warm and cosy feeling
Lots of tender loving care

Happiness enjoys my company
We work well together
We drink shots until we spew
And laugh it off again

Life springs from me
Using up my energy
Taking in my essence
And introducing a plethora of feelings

I cover the outside of the children's ride
Thinking about the knowledge within
Wondering about their future
Contemplating how they have come to get here

My bitterness rages through the mouths of the stupid
Adding a sourness and edge to food
Cleansing the unclean, adding a great scent
I am a colour, but what colour am I?

One Day

One day I noticed that there were two round vents on the wall. Each had a bead of clear liquid rolling down below them. I watched them for ages staring deep into their souls and them looking back into mine. Then suddenly they blinked – yeah, blinked. I ran, and ran, and ran. I sped home and dived under the covers. A while passed, and I peeped out from under the covers. There they were on my wall. They blinked and multiplied over and over again. I sunk back under my covers. Safe… or am I?

I'm asleep now, dreaming of these circles, these blinking circles, these blinking circles coming at me. One hit me, hard. I awoke. Seeing the world in a different light. I wasn't where I fell asleep. Unable to move, I hollered. Nothing happened. I was so high up; I could s-ss-ssss see m-mm-mmyself looking at me from within my English class. Before I knew it, I blinked…

Maariya Saiyed

Crazy. Thoughtful. Caring. Careless. Smart. Stupid. Beautiful. Exciting. Funny. Will tell you the truth even if she knows it will hurt you, so basically she is amazing, and that amazing person is Maariya Saiyed. She was born on the 29th of August 2001 in Hackney. She was raised in Forest Gate. She is currently thirteen and acts like a typical Snapchat-obsessed teenager but she's definitely not typical. When she was first introduced to First Story, straight away she was interested and joined immediately. Creative writing is her way of expressing herself. There are no boundaries. There are no limits. There is just a book, a pen and a couple of mad ideas stored in one little brain. And she loved the fact that nobody was telling her what to write about, she could write freely without being pressured to write a long essay that she felt no excitement about. She is one of a kind, and the most genuine, down to earth girl you would ever have the pleasure of meeting, plus she's a fantastic writer. You'll be lucky to meet someone even a tiny bit like her.

Demon Lover

I was not too keen on her
A precious jewel standing there alone
I could see her through the window
As I leant against my easel, thinking what to do
Knock, knock, knock...

She's liable for knitting
Why?
For stabbing knitting needles into helpless souls
She is a demon
That wants to be loved
But cannot...

Passing by every house
Leaving her seductive scent
Lightly knocking on every door
Possessing everybody in her wake
But never really hurting them...

Chess

I looked under my bed for the chess set. A hand pushed it out. 'What? Isn't that what you wanted?'

My carefree parents had left me alone in the dingy old house, watching TV, since I had nothing else to do. My stomach continuously grumbled at me, forcing me to feed it some food. But as I was a typical lazy teenager, I wasn't bothered to move, so I snacked on some leftover chocolates I found.

Tap, tap, tap…

'SHUT UP, TREES! Can't you see I'm watching TV?' Ugh – 'satellite signal loss' 'Really!?'

So I guess I was down to board games.

I think I have chess upstairs…

The Eyes of the World

I watch things like this every day
But I can't do anything
But watch.
She was grasping on to the one strand of strength she had left
He just took a picture and left.

She wasn't carrion
She was a friend
But the photographer didn't know
He just took a picture and left.

Blaming wildlife for these disgraceful acts
But what do I know
He just took a picture and left.

Blank

Some may say it's boring
Some may say it holds a thousand words
It's un-named
But it's named every day
It's rarely used
But only the rarest of minds can use it
It can be used to its full potential
Or it can make the slightest difference with one streak
It brings peace to the mind
This is the beginning of a whole new world
Never underestimate this colour
Because it's the only colour that can judge you

Blank.

Vidhee Jagatia

The Wagon Wheel Vidhee. Her exterior is tough and delicious but in reality she is as gooey and delicate as a marshmallow. The loud, obnoxious mask she wears daily may intimidate others but the ones that are true to her are allowed the privilege to experience her squidgy side. Growing up in a society and environment of constant conflict and challenges, Vidhee has little interest in limiting herself to what her surroundings have to offer. With an immense passion for Taekwondo, street dance and sports, this amazing soon-to-be woman shares her heart with anyone who is worthy enough. She has an aura that is consistently buzzing from the ecstasy named life. Her journey to First Story was somewhat forced upon her by friends but she learned to use writing as a way to expose her undiscovered skill and to take us on a rollercoaster of words and emotions.

Material = Evil

All I could think about was material things
Possessions, money and all that bling
I needed it, I needed it all
The only way I could get it was by fraud

I had a craving for silver, gold, and platinum
So I went into a shop and attempted to nick some
I tried to walk out
BEEP, BEEP, BEEP
The alarm went off and left me feeling perturbed

Maul was happening the security guard ran over
People were attacking me, I was getting injured
Lifeless I was feeling, I felt myself going
All the material things were defo not worth it!

The Darkest Figure

You know when you feel like there's someone standing over you at night?

Well, if you really saw what it was, you would not feel like your blanket would protect you from it!

Love...
Before you know you're in love
You have to go through hard times.
The person you have affection for
May not always be *Prince Charming*
However much pain you've been through
You have to hold on to time and never give up!
Love isn't simple
There are bumps and obstacles

Before you know you're in love,
You've got to feel that spark,
Every time he walks into the room
You can feel your heart melting
When you stare into each other's eyes,
You can see the twinkle.
Love isn't simple, but it can be *magical*...

The Vulture's Eye

They thought I didn't know,
Of course I knew: I'm not blind!
I could see them sitting there
Waiting, waiting for the right moment
So they can take the perfect photo.
Telling their kind I was going to kill her, but NO!
This wasn't me, this was them.
They call me a wild animal, but in fact they are the real animals.
At least I don't kill my fellow vultures,
I'm not like you!
This is who you are!
'The superior race?'
More like ignorant killers.
Killers of animals, and even their own species
The human race themselves

Nadia Ayiris

Nadia was born and raised in London. She joined First Story because she enjoys poetry which enables her to express her thoughts and feelings perfectly. She is a confident individual and flies through daily progressions. She has a wide range of knowledge and many inspirations that help her succeed. Nadia is thoughtful for others as well as for herself. I feel that her life is well balanced and maintained perfectly. She has become stronger mentally after going through challenges, but she never gave up. In my opinion, she is a really caring human and it's a great thing if you have ever met her!

As Yet Untitled

What to say, what to do, what to write,
Creating a title can be a fright,
It could take up to all night
But when you succeed, you'll be enticed with delight
But for me, it's a whole other world,
In a mind of an abstract girl,
Like me, my head surrounded with frenzy curls
All under that is nothing but an abstract girl, thinking of a motto to conceal her insecurities
Yet the greatest ideas just turn out to be right beside you,
It's about what you say, write and do,
No matter who or what reads this,
It is only what you say, write and do,
That can stop you from being you.

Don't Clone My Bones!

Is it hard to get along?
Can't we just all make amends?
Instead of dying in dead ends,
That's far from a simple approach
According to Annabelle Croach,
Even though we're made to act as one,
We vary from one another,
Just because we're formed under the same roof,
We seek for the truth, and the truth is we're from two very different worlds.
None of them can see the difference in us
They're shallow like the tabloid newspapers
Once the juicy stories have disappeared
They instantly want the rest to disappear in one go
We're constant
Our flaws should be embraced
Not shattered with disgrace
We stand next to one another
Like Marks and Spencer
We all crave for water but blood's thicker.

Urge

I'm paddling for my life,
Trying to rely on the ocean,
It's just reminding me of my emotions
It's gradually trying to scurry me down
Gravitating me down and down
I can't be defeated by my emotions
I glare at the ocean and see myself
My body language, dried out eyes, in line with my horrible,
heavily kohled eyes
I see a small blurry spot

I jump out and swim from it
I swim further; my limbs and arms get heavier and heavier
Like my other half
When I figure out it has been out and about with a juicier,
younger heart
It's like my blood has been brutally sucked out, it's bubbly, and
conscience has faded into separate, individual parts.
I have to pick a side, the robins, mocking jays or the eager eagles
Instead, I am locked in motionless, untimely fare-wellness
Cherish your life and loved ones while you still can,
Because when that's all gone, you'll be desperate to turn the
clock back.

A Warning to the TARDIS

Before you know what the future holds

You need to embrace the present, thank your friends for your company and presence

There are never closed doors; they are always slightly open, even if it's a trigger,

This vow shall remain inside you wherever you go.

The future is under your hands, not in them,

You only have yourself to prove,

So if you ever come by falling off a cliff, pick yourself up because the world isn't going to be waiting for you to get a grip, so keep doing what you're doing because you'll pick up the pieces on the way.

Niamh Carr

Born on 20th November, 2000 at Newham General Hospital, growing up in the urban end of London, an anti-conformist, she is somewhat of an imaginative being. At an early age, she took an interest in art, specifically drawing – nothing in particular but anything that appealed to her interest.

At the age of six, she began to take a big interest in writing and things regarding her future. She dug deep into dark topics of life's harsh truths through her writing.

Her music taste developed very quickly, from bands like Nirvana, which dominated the rock genre throughout the early 90s, to rappers like Eminem who have had a huge impact on music today.

A few years later at secondary school, her life changed very quickly. School is much more challenging, but too serious for her liking. Currently, she faces the challenges of the GCSE curriculum to study for future exams.

Gouge

I'm sorry for faking it. I'm sorry for tearing you apart, covering you with sleeves and asphyxiating you with the mask you chose for the whole world to see. 'I didn't know you'd be insane. Dreams can be so deceiving.' You're 'a wound that won't heal', and even though I've grown to hate your pathetic guts after fourteen years of your existence, I'm sorry that we've learnt to see the world for the hell-hole it really is. I'm sorry you didn't last as long as Kurt did, and I'm sorry you weren't the same media-confined conformist that all these 'happy people' are. But hey, we've been a long way. Even if for more than half of your life we both despised you, you managed to pull off the façade. I'm sorry I have a gun. I'm sorry I'm shoving it down your throat but all that diseased brain was causing was trouble for you. I'm sorry, kid. It was nice knowing you. As your hero once said, 'better to burn out than to fade away.' I'm sorry that this is the end for the both of us.

Bang.

Void

I can symbolise emptiness, yet also be full,
The outlining of the cartoon you adored as an infant,
I give things more… definition.
I'm the fermentation of a mood,
The deterioration of a disturbed child,
The disease and darkness that signifies the
evil within each and every one of you.
I'm the void. The void between appearance and reality,
that can intertwine the two when the time is right.
I'm the original colour. I'm the engulfing gap between bullet
and barrel,
I'm the aftermath when the trigger is pulled,
the spectrum is lost and your head is cascaded
with me.
The coating of an army of crows rising against a horizon of
greens, yellows, blues, reds, purples,
contrasted like a demon among angels.
I'm the sufficient abyss that greets you when
all hope has disintegrated and all you are left with
is the feeling inside,
that you have no release,
your passion has worn down to one final emotion:
Numb.
Because I have infected your veins
with a surge of ink-like poison,
so you are empty, yet full
and I have gouged out the remains
of your innocence,
your sanity.

Thus, whether the trigger is pulled or not,
everything is intricately linked
with me.
The disease. The permanent stain.
The inundation.
The void.

Don't Try to Get It

Before you understand bullying,
you must understand
that for some, the life of a student
is not what you had planned.

Have the secure veil of acceptance
extracted from your veins,
until your joints are cemented
with an inundation of pain.

You say 'get over it,'
as if their insides aren't breaking,
like my ligaments don't shake in
this school torture situation,

where threats are acceptable,
opinion is terrible,
outcasts are despicable,
yet you call this life liveable,

where clinical depression,
is just seeking some attention,
where my ultimate impression
is *society's a prison*,

and at nights, where bigots lay to rest,
we convulse and gasp for breath,
we think this will be our death,
yet you simply do not get,

you will never EVER get,
our sick twisted mentality,
bullying is unforgivable,
you'll always fail in understanding me.

Prey

I am the enemy,
but not the one and only,
I'm the potential catastrophe,
yet there's more to this scenery,

I may be the catastrophe,
but she's awaiting catastrophe,
he caused the catastrophe,
so what more is there to this scene?

The downfall of humanity,
the disregard for suffering,
the glassy camera eye sees
the teamwork in this tragedy,

I'm not the only scum with eyes,
that resemble a heartless void,
she obtains foetal position,
to avoid seeing the invisible coil,

tightening around his throat,
the witness, held back by the noose
that later will consume his airways
when there's nothing left to lose.

Callum

The first question he asked was
'would you like to be buried
or cremated?'
as the school grounds
became a torture base.

The demons had circled.
Their latest demand for dominance,
was to take a hand to my head
and bulldoze it
against the wall.

Where the pretty were vile,
and the outcasts are dying,
where fair is foul,
and foul is fair.

Sohaib Rashid

A flickering flame, silently non-conforming to the engulfing mass among him, day in, day out. Predominantly happy in his lifetime, but frequently falling into blind melancholy spells that remind him of his darkened traits. He took his first gaze into the world on the 9th January 2001 at Whitechapel Hospital, the youngest child of three, yet by far the most human in the sense that he has a wider emotional range. An onset of bullying ensued throughout his early childhood and after years of torment and the abrupt passing of the loved one who was keeping him happy, he has developed a complex understanding of the darkness that undertones the world around us. And that is where his writing comes in…

Death of the Innocence

Why am I still here?
Why is the bird still there?
My body is beginning to shut down,
But why won't you just let me drown?

Why are you standing there? Yes, I mean you, drop your camera, please help, can I take a step and disappear?
Nobody cares and nobody knows,
I refuse to live through this inevitable hell, my throat is dry, my legs are bruised, nobody cares, I should have died when I could.

Drive a blade through my throat,
Make me bleed PLEASE MAKE LIFE STOP,
Don't be ashamed: you'll save this child
Release your anger, release your frustration, make me bleed, I won't mind I won't resist, I can't resist,
Just stop my suffering, I want to rest in peace. You understand, don't you?
Make it stop, show me my end.

We Hope You Enjoy Your Stay at the Robo-Tel

Created, programmed and controlled,
Obedient, simplistic, yet skilled,
The great mechanical robots of Robo-Tel
Here to serve, as long as they're needed.

Morning, afternoon, evening and night,
Work, more work, and even more work,
They don't get tired like we humans do,
Because humans in reality are a dull species,
And yet you would be in luck,
Superior beings serve us inferior beings.

Isn't that just dead boring?
It's boring, everything is simple,
Don't you want to enjoy your stay?
Make your decision, Robo-Tel is a waste,
Shame on those who have already been.

Distorted Mind

His blood was dark,
Tainted, foul, evil and distorted,
It flowed like a waterfall,
Already he has suffered enough,

It was time to meet his inevitable end,
Time to fall into a pit of darkness,
Shut down completely,
Become empty, enter the void,
Leave the horrible universe behind,
Nothing else matters,
It's time to say goodbye,
Time to escape this body,
I am not human, goodbye,

For days I lie in darkness,
Is this the end?
Darkness, emptiness, nothingness,
I await your arrival,
Provide me with doses of satisfaction
Distract me from reality,
Repetitive lifestyles,
They lead to your end